THE PILGRIM VILLAGE MYSTERY

created by
GERTRUDE CHANDLER WARNER

Illustrated by Charles Tang

ALBERT WHITMAN & Company
Morton Grove, Illinois

Z-8332

Activities by Nancy E. Krulik

Activity illustrations by Alfred Giuliani

ISBN 0-8075-6531-8

5 7 9 10 8 6 4

Printed in the U.S.A.

Contents

CHAPTER   PAGE

1. An Emergency Meeting   1
2. Looking for a Mystery   11
3. Smoke!   24
4. All Jumbled Up   39
5. Violet Sees Something   52
6. Angry Voices   66
7. Peanut Butter and Jelly, Please   78
8. Henry's Plan   87
9. Who Wrote the Note?   99
10. Benny Saves the Day   108

CHAPTER 1

An Emergency Meeting

Benny Alden ran into his sister's room. "Jessie! Jessie! Emergency meeting in the boxcar! Come quick!" he called out.

Jessie smiled at her six-year-old brother. "Emergency meeting? What does that mean?"

"It means right away!" Benny said, tugging on his twelve-year-old sister's arm.

"All right, I'm coming," Jessie replied, laughing.

The children went outside to the old boxcar, which was on the lawn behind their grandfather's large house. Ten-year-old Violet and fourteen-year-old Henry were already inside, sitting on the floor.

The boxcar had once been the children's home. When their parents died, Henry, Jessie, Violet, and Benny had run away. They discovered the boxcar in the woods and lived inside it. But then their kind grandfather found them and took them to live with him. As soon as he realized how homesick his grandchildren were for their beloved boxcar, he had it moved to the backyard so they could play in it.

When Jessie and Benny were sitting on the floor, Henry said, "Benny, what's the big emergency?"

"We have another mystery to solve!" Benny exclaimed, his eyes sparkling.

"We do?" Violet asked. "What is it?"

"Well," Benny began, "before he left for work, I saw Grandfather packing his suitcase. And I heard him telling Mrs. McGregor to get *our* suitcases out of the attic and start packing them, too!"

"Oh, Benny, that's no mystery. We must be going on a trip," Violet said. The children took many trips with their grandfather, and each time they found a mystery to solve.

"But where?" asked Benny. "And when?"

"It must be soon," Henry pointed out, "if Grandfather has already started packing."

"Did you ask Mrs. McGregor?" Jessie asked. Mrs. McGregor was their grandfather's housekeeper.

"Yes," Benny replied. "But she wouldn't tell me. She said Grandfather would tell us tonight at dinner."

"Can't you wait until then?" Violet asked.

"But that's such a long time," Benny cried. "It's not even lunchtime yet!"

The others laughed. "Maybe you can solve this mystery before Grandfather gets home," Jessie said.

"All by myself?" Benny asked, frowning.

"You can do it!" Henry assured his brother.

Benny stood up and looked out the door of the boxcar toward the house. Then he turned to his brother and sisters and gave them a big smile. "I'm going to look for clues!" he called, running back to the house.

A few hours later, the children were making lunch. Mrs. McGregor had made a bowl of tuna fish salad, which Henry was spreading on bread. Jessie was pouring cold milk into four large glasses. Benny waited until Mrs. McGregor left the kitchen, then he told the others about the detective work he'd done.

"I looked at the clothes Mrs. McGregor was packing for us," Benny said, his voice low. He was already sitting at the big round table and had started eating his sandwich. Benny loved to eat, and he always had a big appetite.

"And what did you find?" Jessie asked, carrying the glasses of milk to the table.

"She's packed regular clothes — you know, jeans and shirts like we're wearing now," Benny said.

"Then we must not be going anywhere too hot or too cold," Jessie pointed out.

"Did she put in our old clothes, for working on Aunt Jane's farm?" Henry asked, sitting down next to Benny.

"No," Benny answered around a mouthful of tuna fish.

The children all sat quietly eating their sandwiches, wondering where they might be going.

Then Benny remembered something else. "Grandfather's suitcase was laying open on his bed, so I looked to see what he had packed."

"Was there anything unusual?" Henry asked.

"Yes," said Benny, finishing the last bite of his sandwich. "He packed books."

"Grandfather always brings a book when we go on a trip," Jessie answered. "He loves to read."

"Yes, but there wasn't just one book — there were a few. And all of the titles had a name I recognized." Benny looked around at the others. "The name was George . . . um, George Washington, I think," he said uncertainly.

Henry smiled. "Do you know who George Washington was?"

"Wasn't he the first president of the United States?" asked Benny.

"That's right," said Jessie. "Some people call him the father of our country."

"What could he have to do with our trip?" Violet wondered.

"Maybe we're going to meet him," Benny suggested. "Maybe we're going to travel backward in time!" At that, all of the Aldens burst out laughing.

After what seemed like the longest day of his life, Benny was happy to see Mr. Alden pulling into the driveway. "Grandfather, Grandfather!" Benny called, running outside to greet him.

"Well, Benny. What a nice welcome," Grandfather said, giving him a big hug.

"Let me carry your briefcase," Benny said.

"Oh, well, thank you very much," said Mr. Alden, strolling into the house beside his grandson.

Unable to wait any longer, Benny asked, "Do you have something to tell us?"

"Ah . . . is that why you're so excited?" Mr. Alden said, looking down at Benny. "As a matter of fact I do. Why don't you go get Jessie, Henry, and Violet, and I'll tell all of you at once."

When the children were gathered around Grandfather's comfortable chair in the living room, Mr. Alden began speaking. "I have a surprise that I was going to tell you when we sat down to dinner. But somebody already suspects something, and it seems he can't wait." Grandfather reached out and rumpled Benny's hair. "We're going to spend a week visiting a friend of mine named Linda Crawley, and we're leaving tomorrow. Linda works in a very special place called Pilgrim Village. It's a town where everything is just the way it was in America long ago. The people who work there dress in old costumes, and they show visitors — like us — what life was like back then. There are old buildings where they make things like hand-dipped candles and clay pots," Grandfather explained.

"What do they eat?" asked Benny.

"Oh, Benny, you're always thinking about food," Jessie said with a smile.

"That's a good question. They eat old-fashioned foods," answered Mr. Alden. "That means no hamburgers and french fries." To reassure Benny, who looked worried, he added, "They probably have lots of other good things like freshly baked breads and cookies."

"Where will we stay?" Violet wanted to know.

"I'll be staying in a hotel next door," Grandfather replied. "You can stay there, too, if you'd like. Linda has another idea about where you children can stay, but I'll let her tell you about that."

"Very mysterious, Grandfather," said Jessie.

"This place sounds really interesting!" said Henry.

"I think you'll enjoy Pilgrim Village,"

Grandfather told them. "It's also near where George Washington had his headquarters during part of the American Revolution."

"So that's why you had all those books about him!" Benny exclaimed.

Grandfather laughed. "Leave it to my grandchildren, always solving mysteries. But I'm sure there won't be any mystery in Pilgrim Village."

"There might be," Benny said.

"Well, then it's a good thing that you'll be there to solve it," said Grandfather.

CHAPTER 2

Looking for a Mystery

The next morning the Aldens set off bright and early for Pilgrim Village. They drove for most of the day. Finally, Violet spotted a sign. "Look! *Pilgrim Village, five miles.*'"

"Hooray!" shouted Benny, who was tired of sitting in the car.

A few minutes later, the Aldens pulled into a large parking lot.

"Here we are at last," Grandfather said.

The children were happy to get out of the

car and stretch their legs. Grandfather led the way toward a group of small buildings surrounded by a split-rail fence.

"There's the Visitors' Center," Henry said, pointing.

The Aldens entered the small white building and Grandfather went up to the information counter. "Hello," he said to the man behind the counter. "We're here to see Linda Crawley. I'm an old friend — "

"Well, if it isn't James Alden," a voice called out.

The Aldens turned to see a tall woman heading toward them, with a broad grin on her face. She had long dark hair that was braided and then pulled up in a colorful scarf.

"Linda," Mr. Alden said, "how good to see you!"

"And these must be your famous grandchildren," Linda went on.

"Famous?" Benny asked. "I didn't know we were famous."

Linda laughed. "Every time I talk to your grandfather, he tells me more stories of what

you children are up to — helping to restore an old castle, working in a museum. I couldn't wait to meet you."

After Mr. Alden introduced his grand-children, Linda told them a little bit about the village. "This land used to belong to a man named Thomas Heathcliff," Linda be-gan. "He was a farmer back in the 1700s. His farm was passed down through several generations, who kept a few of the buildings intact. About twenty years ago, the last liv-ing member of the family decided to turn the farm into a park where people could learn about history. It was named in honor of the Pilgrims. The first Heathcliffs came over on the *Mayflower*. And that was how Pilgrim Village began."

Linda paused. "Come out to the green, and I'll show you around." She led them outside onto a grassy square surrounded by a dozen small cabins. People walked about, going from one building to another. The Aldens noticed a number of people in old-fashioned colonial clothing. The women were in long

Looking for a Mystery   15

skirts, cotton blouses, and bonnets, the men in knee-length pants, vests and long coats, and shoes with big buckles.

"This area in the middle of town is called the green," Linda went on. "Around the green are shops you might have found in a colonial village. See, there's the candlemaker's shop," she pointed out a building beside them, "and the general store." She motioned to a slightly larger building with a sign over the door that read "Monroe General Store."

"Are all of these the original buildings from long ago?" Jessie asked.

"No," Linda said. "Some are the buildings from Heathcliff's farm. Others were built much later but were made to look just like the old ones."

Linda led them around the ring of buildings, telling the children about each shop. She ended the tour in front of a small building that said "Print Shop." A man with a round friendly face and brown hair pulled back in a pony tail was just closing the door. He was wearing navy blue knee-length pants, white knee socks, and a full white shirt with a long gray vest over it.

"Eric," Linda said. "I'd like you to meet a very old friend of mine, James Alden," she said, gesturing to Grandfather. Eric shook his hand. "And these are his grandchildren, Henry, Jessie, Violet, and Benny. This is Eric Childs."

Eric shook hands with each of the children.

"The Aldens have just arrived, and they'll be staying here for the week," said Linda.

"What do you do here, Mr. Childs?" Mr. Alden asked.

"Please, call me Eric. I'm a historian." Seeing the puzzled look on Benny's face he explained, "I study history — things that happened a long time ago. Here at Pilgrim Village, I run the print shop."

"What's that?" Benny piped up.

"It's where books, newspapers, and posters are printed," Eric said. "Come by tomorrow and I'll show you. Would you like that?"

"We sure would," Jessie said, answering for all of them.

"Why don't you join us for dinner at the tavern?" Linda asked Eric.

"I'd love to," he said, walking with them across the green.

"Your grandfather has told me what good workers you are," Linda told the children as they walked. "So I've been thinking, instead of just visiting Pilgrim Village, how about really being a part of it? Each day you can help out in one of the shops. You'll learn how to print, weave, make pottery, just the way they used to long ago. What do you think?"

The children's sparkling eyes and eager smiles answered Linda's question, even before Henry said, "That sounds great!"

"There's a cabin right here on the green where you can stay, and I'll give you costumes to wear," Linda added.

"See," cried Benny. "We *are* going back in time!"

The children were very excited about helping out at Pilgrim Village. Grandfather also thought it was a wonderful idea. But when Violet looked over at Eric, he didn't seem pleased. He was walking very slowly, and had a strange look on his face, as if something were bothering him.

Violet was about to ask him what was wrong, when Linda said, "Here's someone else I'd like you to meet." A woman with wavy reddish-brown hair was crossing the green. "This is the newest member of our staff, Shelly August. She starts work tomorrow." Linda introduced each of the Aldens, and then Eric. As Shelly stretched out her hand to shake his, Violet noticed that her beautifully manicured nails matched her red suit perfectly.

"Shelly," Eric said stiffly. "Pleased to meet you."

"Nice to meet you also," Shelly said with a polite smile.

"I'm sorry but I must be going now," Eric said. He turned abruptly and began walking back toward the print shop.

"I thought you were going to have dinner with us," Linda called out.

"Yes, well . . . there's something I have to take care of. . . ." He walked quickly away without another word.

"I'd better be going, too," Shelly said. "Big day tomorrow!" She headed off in the opposite direction.

"That was odd, wasn't it?" Jessie said. "Eric seemed to be having such a nice time, and then suddenly he wasn't."

"Yes, and did you notice how he and Shelly looked at each other? Almost as if they already knew each other," added Violet.

"That's impossible," Linda said. "They would have said something."

"Not if they didn't want anyone to know," Henry said.

"But why wouldn't they want anyone to know?" Linda looked puzzled.

"Don't worry." Mr. Alden chuckled. "My grandchildren are always looking for mysteries to solve. I'm sure it's nothing. Let's go eat. I'm getting hungry, and I know I'm not the only one." Grandfather grinned at Benny.

"I'm starving!" Benny said.

Grandfather put his arm around Benny and gave him a squeeze. "That's my Benny!" he said.

"Then let's get going!" Linda led them across the green and into a large building with a sign that said "Red's Tavern." The restaurant was filled with people. Everyone seemed to be talking and laughing, enjoying themselves. Candles flickered on the long wooden tables, and at the far end of the room a fire crackled in a large stone fireplace.

"Mmmm!" Benny said. "It sure smells good in here."

"Yes, it does," Jessie agreed.

"And just wait until you taste Red's cooking," Linda told them. "He's been the cook here since Pilgrim Village opened."

A waitress in a long skirt led the Aldens to a table. "Hi, I'm Lisa. Welcome to Red's Tavern." She pointed to a chalkboard over the fireplace. "There's the menu. What can I bring you?"

"The chicken pot pie is Red's specialty," Linda said.

"Sounds good to me." Grandfather looked around the table at the children, who nodded their heads in agreement. "We'll all have chicken pot pie."

When the food arrived, everyone ate eagerly. The Aldens had ~~had~~ a long day of traveling, and the hot chicken stew was delicious. It had big chunks of chicken, potatoes, and carrots, and a light, flaky crust. For dessert, there was warm apple pie.

When the last bite of pie had been eaten, Grandfather sat back in his chair. "What a delicious meal. The chef is wonderful!"

"I'm so glad you feel that way," Linda said. "Excuse me a moment." She got up and headed to the far side of the restaurant and through a swinging door. In no time she was back, and beside her was a large man with gray hair and a gray beard. A clean white apron stretched across his round belly.

"So these are the Aldens," the man said. "Linda told me to cook up something special for you."

"Are you the cook?" Jessie asked.

"Sure am. Red Sullivan at your service," he said.

"The food was great," said Henry.

"Glad to hear it, my boy," replied Red.

"Is Red really your name?" Benny wanted to know.

"It's my nickname. I used to have bright red hair, back when I was your age," Red explained.

"When you first came here your hair was red," Linda pointed out.

"That was a long time ago," Red said thoughtfully, stroking his beard. "Pilgrim Village was just a quiet little place then."

"It certainly isn't quiet anymore," Henry said, looking around the tavern.

"You should see it at Thanksgiving," Red said. "But that is a few weeks away, so I guess you won't be here."

"Isn't it wonderful how popular the village has become?" Linda said proudly. "In fact, if we keep doing this well, we may be able to expand."

"I don't think it's so wonderful," said Red. "We don't need more tour buses filling up the parking lot, dumping even more people on us."

"Oh, Red," Linda said. "You don't mean that."

"Yes, I do," Red insisted, his face flushing.

"Maybe we could help you in the kitchen," Violet said, trying to change the subject. "You could show us how you make that delicious apple pie." The children had cooked while they were living in the boxcar, and they still enjoyed making meals for themselves.

"I don't need more tourists," Red said angrily, "and I certainly don't need any children in *my* own kitchen!" He turned and headed back to the kitchen in a huff.

CHAPTER 3

Smoke!

"Why'd he get so upset?" Jessie asked as the Aldens got up from their table and left the tavern.

Linda sighed. "It's not your fault. Lately Red has just been a little bit . . . touchy. I don't know what's bothering him."

"We'll cheer him up!" Benny said.

"I hope you can. But in the meantime I'd better get you children settled," Linda said. "I'll take you back to your cabin and give you your costumes."

The Aldens stopped at their car and got their suitcases. Then they went with Linda to a small log cabin at one end of the green. There was a lantern on the front steps. Linda lit the lantern with a match, and led the children inside. By the flickering light of the lantern, the children saw they were in a square room. Across from the door was a large stone hearth with a cast iron pot hanging in the center. A simple wooden table stood in the middle of the room. On either side of the room was a door leading into two smaller rooms.

"Jessie and Violet can sleep here," Linda said, leading the children into the small room on the left. There was a double bed with a wooden frame, fluffy pillows, and a patchwork quilt pulled over it. "And the room on the other side has a double bed for you and Henry," Linda told Benny.

"Did Thomas Heathcliff live here?" asked Benny.

"No, he lived in the farmhouse at the other end of the village," Linda said. "This little cabin was for his guests. And it's still used just for extra-special guests."

"It's wonderful!" cried Violet.

"It reminds me of the boxcar days," said Benny.

"If you need anything, I sleep in the apartment over my office, which is right next door," Linda said.

"We'll be fine," Jessie assured her. "We like being on our own."

"Now that you're settled, I'm going back to my hotel," Grandfather said. "I'll meet you at the tavern at lunchtime tomorrow."

"See you!" Benny said, giving his grandfather a big hug.

"Good night!" the other children called out as Linda and Grandfather closed the door behind them.

The Aldens woke up the next morning to sunlight streaming through the tiny windows of their cabin. Linda had given them colonial costumes the night before, and the children put them on excitedly. The blouses and skirts fit Jessie and Violet perfectly. "Look how cute you look!" Jessie said, helping Violet tie on her bonnet.

Benny put on his shirt and his breeches, which were a little bit too long. "These were the smallest pair Linda could find," Henry said.

Jessie rolled the breeches up at the waist, and fastened them with safety pins she had in her suitcase. She was very organized and always came prepared.

Henry looked quite handsome in his blue breeches and vest. "Don't forget your hat, Benny." He handed his brother the three-cornered hat. Benny had just finished buckling his shoes, and was jumping about in his new outfit.

Linda had told them to go to the print shop that morning and help Eric.

"What about breakfast?" Benny asked as he helped Jessie smooth the quilts over the beds.

"Remember we saw that little bakery yesterday? We can get something there," Violet suggested.

"But I don't remember where it was," Benny said, following the others out of the cabin.

"I think we should be able to find it pretty easily," Jessie said, breathing in deeply.

"We'll just follow our noses!" said Henry.

Sure enough, the Aldens could smell something delicious drifting their way. They walked toward the scent, and soon found themselves in front of the small bake shop. Over the door hung a wooden sign shaped like a loaf of bread, and through the window they could see baskets of fresh-baked rolls and muffins on the countertop.

Each of the Aldens bought a muffin: corn for Jessie, cranberry for Henry and Violet, and blueberry for Benny. The woman behind the counter also sold them cups of milk, although she explained that in colonial times, they would have had to milk their own cow.

"I'm glad we don't have to do that," Benny said.

The Aldens sat on a bench outside the bakery and ate the warm muffins and drank the cold milk.

After breakfast, they headed to the print shop, which was on the other side of the green. The children wondered if Eric would be as friendly as he had been when they'd first met him. When he'd left them the night before he hadn't seemed friendly at all.

The Aldens were relieved to find that he was happy to see them. "Welcome!" Eric said cheerfully. "Ready to learn about printing?"

"We sure are!" said Henry.

"First put these on so that you don't get ink on your clothes." Eric handed each of the children a large, heavy apron. "Today I'm printing posters to advertise a special harvest picnic this Saturday at noon on the green. There will be lots of games and prizes, and plenty of food, of course. But before we can start printing, we need to decide what the posters should say, and how they should look."

Eric set the children up at a table with some paper and pencils, while he talked to some visitors who had just come in. When at last the Aldens had agreed on the design, they showed it to Eric.

You're invited!
HARVEST PICNIC ON THE GREEN
Contests, games, prizes, and plenty of food
Saturday at twelve o'clock
Please come and enjoy the fun!

"That looks great," Eric said. "Now for the next step." He pulled out two large flat wooden cases. The cases were divided into lots of little compartments that were filled with metal blocks. Eric reached in the top case and took a block from the upper left-hand compartment. On one side of the block was the letter A. "You see, each of these blocks has a letter on it. This upper case holds the capital letters. The lower case holds the small letters."

"Is that why they're called 'upper case' and 'lower case' letters?" Jessie asked.

"Yes, as a matter of fact, it is," said Eric. "These are called blocks of type. You'll take the type from these cases and lay them in this metal tray." He showed them an empty metal tray on the counter. "First you'll need a capital Y for 'You're' and then a small o and a small u and so on. Once all of the type is arranged in this tray, you roll ink over the tray, and put the tray in the printing press." He motioned to a large machine. "But I'll show you how to do that later."

"Is this really how they printed all their newspapers and books and everything?" Henry asked.

"Yes," Eric said. "Things were a lot harder then. But before you start arranging the letters in the tray, there's one important thing you have to remember. The letters have to be put in backward."

"Backward!" Violet said.

"Let me show you," Eric said. He took a few pieces of type out of the cases, and laid them in the tray. "Know what that says?" The children leaned over to see. Eric had placed the letters ɅИ∃B in the tray, and they were all backward. Then he inked the tray and put it in the press. After he'd printed a page, he showed it to the children.

"That's my name!" Benny said proudly.

"Yes, it is," Eric said. "To check that you've put the type in properly, you use a mirror. If the letters are the right way in the mirror, they'll come out right on the paper. In colonial times, boys no older than Violet might have had a job like this. Do you know who Benjamin Franklin was?"

"Is he the one who discovered electricity with a kite and a key?" Benny asked.

"He was indeed," said Eric. "And he started off as an apprentice in his brother's print shop doing the same kinds of things you'll be doing."

For the rest of the morning the children laid the blocks of type in the tray. There were several different cases of type, large and small, fancy and plain. It was fun deciding how the poster should look.

While the Aldens worked, more visitors came into the shop, and Eric explained what the children were doing and demonstrated how the printing press worked.

At about noon, Benny's stomach began to growl. "Can we take a break for lunch?" he asked.

"Sure," said Eric. "You can finish the poster later."

"We're supposed to meet Grandfather at the tavern. Would you like to come along with us?" Jessie asked Eric.

"Sounds great," he said. Then a look passed over his face as if he'd just remembered something. "Oh, no, on second thought . . . I have a special project I have to work on."

"What is it?" Benny asked.

"Well, it's . . . it's . . . uh . . ." Eric began. "It's really nothing."

"Then why do you have to — " Benny said.

"Come on, Benny," Henry interrupted his brother. "Let's give Eric some time to himself."

The tavern was just as busy as it had been the night before. Mr. Alden was waiting at a table in the corner, and he'd already ordered the special — fried chicken and biscuits — for all of them. They told him about their morning at the print shop and he was very impressed.

The Aldens were just biting into the crispy

chicken when they heard a commotion at the back of the restaurant. Next, they saw black smoke coming from the kitchen. The people sitting near the kitchen door were jumping up from their tables, coughing and waving the smoke away with their hands.

"Uh-oh!" cried Violet. "Looks like trouble in the kitchen."

"Maybe Red could use some help," Henry suggested. He led the others to the kitchen door and poked his head in. The kitchen was filled with smoke. Red stood next to the stove, holding two large trays of biscuits that had been burnt to a crisp. Their waitress from the night before, Lisa, and a waiter whose nametag said "Steve" were hurrying about the kitchen, opening windows to clear the smoke.

"What happened, Red?" Henry asked.

"I don't know. Someone must have turned off my timer, so I didn't take the biscuits out when I should have." Red looked at one of the knobs on the stove. "What is this doing set at four hundred and fifty degrees? No wonder these burned."

"Everyone's ordering the special chicken and biscuits," said Lisa. "And now we're out of biscuits."

Steve looked out into the dining room, where angry voices could be heard. "Several of the customers are upset about all the smoke. We're going to lose a lot of business if we don't do something fast."

"We can help," Violet offered.

Red looked angry. "I don't need any help!"

"Why not, Red?" Lisa asked. "Steve and I are having trouble keeping up with all the customers as it is."

"Well, all right," Red said reluctantly. He didn't seem happy.

"I'll go open the windows in the dining room and fan out some of the smoke," Jessie said.

"I'll tell the customers not to worry, that their lunches will be served soon," said Henry.

"What can I do?" asked Benny.

"You and I can help Red make more biscuits," said Violet.

No sooner had the children spoken than

they got to work. Red got out large containers of flour, shortening, baking powder and milk. Following Red's instructions, Violet carefully measured the ingredients into a bowl, and Benny stirred the mixture with a wooden spoon. Then they placed spoonfuls of batter on a baking sheet, and Red put the sheet in the oven. He checked the temperature and timer carefully.

In no time the biscuits were done, and the children helped arrange them on plates next to Red's crispy fried chicken. Lisa and Steve rushed the meals out to the customers.

Seeing that things seemed to be running smoothly, the children returned to their table, where Grandfather was waiting for them.

"Thanks a lot," Steve called out.

Red said nothing.

After the Aldens had finished eating, the children said good-bye to Grandfather, who was planning to take a nap in his hotel room, and walked back to the print shop. As they strolled across the green, Jessie said, "Red didn't seem very grateful for our help."

"No, he didn't," said Henry.

"Don't you think it was strange that both the timer and the temperature on the oven were set wrong?" Violet asked.

"Red seemed to think someone had changed the settings," said Jessie.

"Do you think someone wanted those biscuits to burn?" Benny asked, his eyes wide.

"Why would anyone want that?" said Violet. "It just made a lot of people unhappy." Violet hated to think of anyone being unhappy.

"I don't know," said Henry. "But something about what happened just doesn't seem right."

CHAPTER 4

All Jumbled Up

When the children returned to the print shop, they found Eric's assistant, Judith, giving demonstrations for the visitors. "Eric's in his office," she told them.

"I'll tell him we're back," Violet said, walking to Eric's office at the back of the shop. When she entered the small room, Eric was sitting at his desk, his head bent over a book. The book looked very old. Violet could see that the pages were yellowed and the cover was made of leather that was cracked around the edges. The book was handwrit-

ten, and there were blots of ink here and there on the page. Eric was so busy making notes on a pad of paper that he didn't realize Violet had come in.

"Eric," she said softly. Since he still didn't look up, she said his name again, louder.

"What?" Eric looked around, startled. Seeing Violet, he quickly closed the book as if he didn't want her to see it and put it into a drawer with the pad of paper. "Oh, hello." He stood up and ushered Violet out of his office.

"Was that your special project?" Violet didn't want to be nosy, but she was very curious about the old book.

"Uh, yes . . ." Eric said nervously. Then he quickly changed the subject. "How was your lunch?"

"It was good, except there was a little problem in the tavern." Violet was about to tell Eric what had happened when a large group of tourists entered the shop. Eric went to help Judith demonstrate the printing process.

By the end of the afternoon, the shop was quiet again. Since there weren't many visitors, Judith left early. The Aldens completed the tray of type for their poster and checked it carefully in the mirror. Then they showed it to Eric.

"Great work," he said. "We'll print it tomorrow."

"Why not today?" Jessie asked.

"You've done enough work. Go enjoy yourselves," Eric insisted.

"We are enjoying ourselves," Henry replied.

Eric looked at the children as if he didn't know what to say. Then he seemed to have an idea. "You know, the general store sells delicious apple cider. Have you tried it yet?"

"No," said Henry. "But — "

"I think Benny would really like it," said Eric, guiding the Aldens out the door. "We'll print your poster tomorrow."

"Okay," said Jessie. "But what about our aprons?" She had begun untying hers.

"Bring them back tomorrow. Bye!" The

children were surprised when Eric quickly shut the door and turned the sign in the window around so that it said "Closed."

"He certainly seemed in a hurry to get rid of us," Henry commented.

"Yes, he did," Violet agreed. "I wonder if he's going to work on his special project. When I went into his office after lunch, he was looking at a very old book. As soon as he saw me, he put the book away so I couldn't see what it was."

"First Red acted strange, and now Eric. What's going on?" asked Benny.

"I don't know," said Jessie. "But that cider sounds pretty good to me. Let's go."

The Aldens arrived at the print shop the following morning, ready to print their poster. Eric welcomed them in, but he seemed very distracted.

He showed them how to place the tray of type in the printing press. Then he took out a large roller and showed them how to coat it with sticky, black ink.

"Jessie, why don't you roll the ink over the type," Eric suggested.

Then Eric showed Violet where to put the first sheet of paper.

"Henry, press down on this bar here," Eric said.

"Here we go," said Henry, following Eric's instructions. The sheet of paper was pressed firmly against the tray of type.

Carefully Jessie removed the first poster from the press.

"Let me see it!" Benny called out.

"Careful," Jessie warned. "The ink's still wet."

Benny turned over the sheet, careful not to put his fingers in the wet ink. The others watched his eyes grow wide. "Uh-oh! I think we goofed."

"What do you mean, Benny?" Jessie asked.

Benny turned the poster around so they could all see it.

StdRn!nu'ldyfoo

read the first line of the poster. The rest of

the poster was just as bad. All of the letters were jumbled around and mixed up — forward, backward, right side up, and upside down.

"What happened?" Violet asked. "We were so careful to put the letters in the right way."

"And we checked it with a mirror, just like Eric showed us," Jessie added.

They were very disappointed. After all their hard work, their poster was a mess.

Henry pulled the tray out of the press and looked at it. The blocks of type were all mixed up. "We'll have to do it over again," Henry said. "I wonder what happened."

Eric was just as puzzled as the children about the mix-up with their poster. "It seems as if someone took all the type out of the tray and rearranged it."

"But you closed the shop right after we finished it," Jessie said.

"Do you think someone came in?" Henry asked.

"Why would someone want to ruin our poster?" Benny wanted to know.

The children noticed that Eric had a strange look on his face, but he didn't answer their questions.

"I guess we'd better get back to work," said Jessie.

By noon the children had fixed the type and printed several copies of their poster.

"You've done a great job," Eric told them. "Now, why don't you go see some more of Pilgrim Village?"

"Are you trying to get rid of us?" Benny asked.

"No, no, of course not." Eric forced a smile. "I just wouldn't want you to miss out on all the other things here."

"Let us know if you need any more help," Jessie said as the Aldens removed their aprons and headed out onto the green.

"It's such a beautiful day," Violet said. "I feel like a picnic."

"Let's go to the snack bar and get some sandwiches," Jessie suggested. The snack bar was one of the few places in the village where people could buy things they didn't have long ago — like hot dogs and hamburgers.

After they finished their lunch, the children went to the pottery shop to see if they could give Shelly a hand.

The pottery shop was set back off the green, surrounded by tall pine trees. When the children entered the building, they found Shelly sitting in a chair, reading a book. She was dressed in a colonial costume, a long blue skirt and full white blouse with an apron on top, and a white bonnet on her head.

"Hello," Henry called out.

Shelly looked up and smiled at the children. "Welcome to the pottery shop. What can I do for you?"

"We're here to make some pots," said Benny.

"I'm sorry. You can't make any today. The clay's all dried out," Shelly said.

"How did that happen?" Violet asked.

"It seems someone left the bags open, and now the clay's ruined. I've ordered more, but it won't be delivered for a week."

"Couldn't you add water to the clay to remoisten it?" Jessie asked.

"Add water? Oh, uh, yes . . . I suppose

you could but . . ." Shelly paused. "It's too late, anyway. I've already thrown the clay away." Shelly could tell the children were very disappointed to hear this news.

"Even though you don't have any clay, can you show us how the potters would sit at the pottery wheel while they worked?" Violet asked. She liked doing all kinds of art, but had never tried pottery.

"Oh, yes, um . . ." Shelly looked at the wheel and the small stool next to it. "They'd sit sort of like this." She sat down and leaned forward awkwardly over the wheel. "See?" When the children all nodded, she got up quickly and led the children to the back of the shop. "The kiln is back here."

"What's that?" Benny asked.

"It's a big oven that bakes the clay until it's hard," Shelly explained.

"How hot does the kiln get?" Henry asked.

"Very hot," Shelly said with a smile. "Much hotter than a regular oven."

"What temperature?" Jessie asked.

"What temperature?" Shelly repeated.

"Oh, uh . . . let me just check my notes over here . . ." She hurried over to a table in the corner. "What temperature," she muttered to herself as she shuffled through the pages. "Isn't that funny. I can't seem to find it." She flipped through the pile one more time. At last she said, "Come back tomorrow and I'll give you the answer."

"What — " Benny began, but Shelly cut him off.

"This is silly, since I don't have any clay to demonstrate for you. Why don't you kids come back later this week and I'll show you how to make a pot," Shelly said.

"But I just wanted to ask — " Benny started again when the door of the shop opened and a couple entered.

"More visitors!" Shelly said. "Excuse me. See you in a few days!" She hurried to greet the new visitors, her skirt swishing as she moved.

The children left the pottery shop feeling puzzled.

"What is it about this place?" Henry asked

as they walked back toward the center of the village. "It seems everyone wants to get rid of us!"

"And another thing," Jessie pointed out. "Shelly didn't seem to know very much about pottery."

"She didn't look very comfortable sitting at the pottery wheel," Benny remarked.

"I was surprised she had to check her notes to answer our questions," Violet added.

"I can't help wondering," said Henry, "who left the bags open so the clay would dry out?"

The children had now reached the middle of the green.

"A lot of things in this village just don't make sense," Jessie said.

"What's this?" Benny asked as the Aldens passed a large yellow building.

"The sign says it's Thomas Heathcliff's farmhouse," Jessie said.

"Remember, Linda told us that he lived there with his family a long time ago," Henry reminded them. "The building next to it must be the stable. She said he really loved his horses."

There was a yard beside the stable surrounded by a split rail fence. In the yard stood a beautiful chestnut horse. As soon as Benny saw the horse, he ran over and climbed up on the fence. "Hello, horsey!"

"That's Betsy," said a man in overalls coming out of the stable. "Isn't she beautiful?"

"She sure is," said Benny.

"I'm Roger," the stable man introduced himself. "How would you kids like to help me out in the stable?"

"That'd be great!" Benny said eagerly. The Aldens spent the rest of the afternoon with Roger, helping him care for the horses.

CHAPTER 5

Violet Sees Something

The next morning, the children joined Linda for a delicious bacon and egg breakfast at the tavern.

"What are we going to do today?" Benny asked when they were finished eating.

"How about the candlemaker's?" Linda suggested.

"That sounds fun," Jessie said.

Minutes later the children were entering a small building that smelled of melted wax.

"Hello, I'm Martha. Would you like to learn how to make candles?" asked a pretty woman in a long flowered dress. Her soft brown hair was pulled back in a thick braid down her back.

"We sure would," said Benny, always eager to learn something new.

"Great! Here's what you do. Take a wick," Martha said, handing each of the children a short stick with a piece of string tied in the center. "Hold your stick and dip the wick into this pot of melted wax. Be careful — the wax is very hot."

One by one, the Aldens did as Martha said. When the wicks were pulled out of the hot wax, each one was coated in a thin layer of wax.

"This doesn't look like a candle," Benny complained.

"Wait a couple of seconds for the wax to cool and harden a bit. Then dip it in again. It takes a while before you build up enough wax to make a candle." The children dipped and cooled their candles again and again while Martha told them about colonial times. She explained how the colonists made the wax by melting down animal fat in a big pot.

They might add scents by mixing in different kinds of berries. But this was only done for special occasions and holidays, because so many berries were needed, and collecting all those berries took a long time.

"I like picking berries," Benny said, thinking of the wild raspberries they sometimes found in Grandfather's backyard.

"Yes, and you also like eating them," added Jessie.

At last Benny pulled out his string and saw that the glob of wax on it was becoming round and thick. "Now it looks like a candle."

Martha smiled at him. "Yes it does. Hang it on this rack." Benny followed her instructions. "When the wax has cooled and hardened you'll be able to cut the wick off the stick. Then you'll have a candle."

"What's this?" Henry asked, picking up a metal object with lots of long hollow tubes.

"It's a candle mold. If you want to make a lot of candles, that's a much easier way to do it. You pour the hot wax into the tubes and let it cool. When you take the candles out of the mold, they are much smoother and more even than the hand-dipped kind," Martha explained.

"Why did they need so many candles?" Benny asked.

"They didn't have electricity back then, Benny," Martha told him. "So they needed candles to see by at night."

While Martha was talking, she was slowly stirring the pot of wax with a large spoon. Violet sat beside her, watching the wax swirl around in the pot. Suddenly she spotted something. "What was that?" she said almost to herself.

"What was what?" Martha asked.

"I think I saw something floating in the wax," Violet said.

"Are you sure?" Martha looked puzzled. "There shouldn't be anything in there but wax."

"I saw a lump," Violet said.

"It was probably just a lump of wax," Martha said.

"No, it looked different," Violet insisted. The other Aldens came over as Martha slowly pulled the spoon through the thick wax and peered into the pot.

"Yes, there it is!" Violet cried out.

"Now I see it," Martha said, carefully scooping something up in the spoon and taking it out of the pot. "Watch out, that wax is very hot," she said as she dumped the spoonful on the wooden counter. The children gathered closer to see what had been in the pot. As the wax dripped away, they saw that it was a pin, the kind that might be worn on a man's tie or a woman's blouse.

"That's very odd." Martha ran a hand over her thick braid. "What's that doing in my pot of wax?"

"May I see it?" Jessie asked.

Martha handed the pin to Jessie, who turned it over carefully in her hand.

"Do you think it belongs to a man or a woman?" asked Henry.

"I don't know," said Jessie. "But this design looks familiar. I've seen it somewhere before, but I can't remember where."

"How could that pin have gotten into the wax?" asked Violet.

"I can't imagine," said Martha. "I just made up this batch of wax yesterday afternoon. A few people came by and made candles, but I was standing right here the whole time. I'd have seen if anything fell in the pot."

"Unless someone came in later, after you'd gone," said Henry.

"Why would someone come in here after hours?" asked Martha. "This is very strange. I'll have to report it to Linda. Would you children like to make any more candles?"

"No," said Henry. "But thanks for showing us how."

"That's what I'm here for," Martha said. She cleaned the wax from the pin and wrapped it in her handkerchief. "I'll go show this to Linda later on."

"Hey, what's happening on the green?" called Benny from the window.

"It's Tuesday, the day of the farmer's market," Martha said.

The other Aldens looked outside and saw a lively market in the center of the village. While they had been working on their candles, local farmers and bakers had set up tables where they were selling all kinds of fruits, vegetables, cheeses, and baked goods.

"You should get something to eat," Martha suggested. "Everything is always fresh and delicious."

"Yes, let's!" Benny said.

"Don't forget to come back later and pick up your candles once they've cooled," Martha called after the Aldens.

The children bought fruit and cheese and a loaf of bread and sat on the green eating their picnic lunch. "The vegetables those farmers are selling look so fresh," Jessie said. "We could buy some and make our own dinner tonight."

"What a good idea," said Henry. "We'll cook just the way the colonists used to."

First the children stopped in Linda's office to make sure it was okay that they cooked in the cabin.

"As long as you're careful and clean up everything," Linda said. "And one other thing."

"What?" asked Violet.

"You invite me," Linda said with a smile.

"Please come for dinner," Violet said.

"Yes, we would love that," said Jessie. "Could we use your phone to call Grandfather and invite him, too?"

Mr. Alden was eager to eat at his grandchildren's cabin. He knew what good cooks they were.

Linda lent them some pewter dishes and utensils, and told them they could use the big kettle in the fireplace.

After speaking with Grandfather, the children were ready to start shopping. They bought carrots, onions, potatoes, and some fresh green herbs at the outdoor market, and also a jug of cider to drink and some fruit for dessert. Then they walked up the street to a modern grocery store to get some meat.

"I'm glad we don't have to hunt for meat the way the early colonists would have," said Henry.

*   *   *

Back at the cabin, Jessie took some logs from the woodpile in back of the cabin and made a fire in the fireplace. Benny and Violet washed and peeled the potatoes and carrots and cut them into small pieces. Henry chopped the beef into chunks. Then he cut up the onions, and their strong smell made his eyes water.

Once the fire was going, Jessie put a little bit of oil in the kettle and browned the chunks of beef. Violet added the vegetables and some water, and seasoned the stew with the herbs.

While the stew cooked, the children straightened up the cabin and set the table. Jessie gathered the potato and carrot peelings and the onion skins and threw them away. Henry placed the plates and glasses around the table and laid the silverware. Violet picked some wildflowers and put them in a little jar in the middle of the table. Benny went to the candlemaker's shop to pick up their candles.

Then there was nothing to do but wait for

the stew to finish cooking. The children sat on the front step of their cabin while they waited. Every once in a while Jessie would tend the fire, or Henry would stir the stew with a long wooden spoon.

Mr. Alden and Linda arrived promptly at six, and were impressed with how pretty the table looked in the little cabin.

"Something smells good," said Grandfather.

"Beef stew!" Benny said. "And we made it just the way they did a long time ago."

"It's getting dark," said Jessie. "I'll light some candles." She took two pewter candlestick holders from the mantle and put in two candles they had dipped themselves that morning. Then she placed the candlesticks in the middle of the table and lit them. A soft glow filled the room.

"We made those candles ourselves, Grandfather," Benny said proudly.

"You did? That's wonderful," Mr. Alden said.

Violet poured a large glass of apple cider for everyone. Henry spooned beef stew onto everyone's plate. "Let's eat," Benny said.

Mr. Alden was the first to take a taste. "This is delicious."

"It's as good as the beef stew Red serves at the tavern," Linda said.

Linda and the Aldens talked and ate, enjoying the tasty stew.

"Martha, the candlemaker, came to me today, and said you'd found something in the wax, Violet." Linda said.

"A pin," said Violet.

"*In* the wax?" Grandfather asked.

"Yes," said Linda. "That's what's so strange. Martha doesn't know how it got there."

"Someone must have come in after she left for the night," said Jessie.

"But why would anyone do that?" asked Linda.

"You know, something strange happened in the print shop, too," Jessie recalled. "We had arranged the type for a poster and left the tray on the counter overnight. In the morning the type was all jumbled up."

"Maybe someone had come in after the

shop was closed, knocked over the tray, and then just put the type back in any which way," Henry said.

"Who would be sneaking into the shops at night?" Linda said. "And why?"

"Well, it doesn't sound too serious so far. No one's reported anything missing, have they?" Grandfather asked.

"No," said Linda. "I guess we'll just have to wait and see. If anything else happens, I might have to get a security guard at night."

As the candles burned lower, Jessie sliced some pears, and Linda set out a tin of short-bread she had brought. Everyone munched on the delicious cookies and juicy slices of pear.

After dessert, Violet and Benny cleared all the dishes and silverware from the table. Grandfather helped Henry wash the dishes and Linda helped Jessie dry them. Soon everything was clean.

Benny let out a big, loud yawn, which made everyone laugh.

"I think it's time somebody got to bed. We'd better go," Grandfather said.

"Thanks for the delicious meal," said Linda.

When their guests had left, the children washed up and put on their pajamas. Then they snuggled into their cozy beds and were soon asleep.

CHAPTER 6

Angry Voices

When the children woke up the next morning, they dressed in their colonial costumes and then stopped at the bakery for muffins.

"Let's go to the weaving shop today," Violet said. "I'd like to learn how to spin thread and make cloth." Violet enjoyed sewing and was very handy with a needle and thread.

Benny made a face. "I want to go see the horses again."

"We did that yesterday," Violet said.

"Yes, but — " Benny began.

"We don't all have to stick together," Henry pointed out.

"Maybe while Henry and Violet go to the weaving shop, we could visit the farmyard," Jessie suggested.

"Okay!" said Benny eagerly.

So the children headed off in two different directions.

But when Henry and Violet reached the weaving shop, they were in for a surprise. Although everything else in the village was open and bustling with activity, the sign in the window of the weaving shop said "Closed."

Henry and Violet saw a movement in the shop, so they peeked through the window. Linda was inside with a man they didn't recognize. When Linda saw the children at the door, she opened it and let them in.

As soon as the children saw the look on Linda's face, they knew something was wrong. Violet was just about to ask what, when Linda stepped back to let them enter the shop, and they saw for themselves. The shop was a mess! The spinning wheel and

the loom had been tipped over and lay on the floor, and there were piles of thread and fabric everywhere.

"What happened?" asked Henry, his eyes wide.

"We don't know," said Linda. "When Arnold, the weaver, came in this morning, the shop looked like this."

"Was it a burglar?" Henry asked.

"It looks like it," said Arnold. "But there's nothing valuable here to steal, and I don't see anything missing."

"The candlemaker's shop, the print shop, and now here. I wonder what's going on," said Henry.

Linda looked very upset. "And there's more. I've been getting complaints about the tavern. Apparently the food and the service haven't been very good. I don't know what's happening. Just when our little village seemed to be doing so well, suddenly everything's falling apart."

"Don't worry, Linda," Violet said. "We'll help you figure out what's going on."

Linda smiled at the children. "I hope you can," she said. "Before it's too late."

Henry and Violet helped Linda and Arnold set the loom and spinning wheel upright. Then they picked up the piles of thread and fabric and sorted them by color.

"Why don't you take the day off," Linda suggested to Arnold when everything was back in its place.

"Thanks. I think I will," Arnold said. "And thank you for your help," he said to Violet and Henry.

"You're welcome," Violet said. "Maybe we can come back another day and learn about weaving."

She and Henry left the shop and headed toward the stable. Benny and Jessie were inside, patting the chestnut horse. Henry told them what had happened at the weaving shop, and how upset Linda was.

"That's terrible," Jessie said. "Do you think this has anything to do with the other strange things that have been happening?"

"I don't know," said Henry.

The Aldens started to walk back toward the green and passed the general store.

"Let's take a look in here," said Violet.

The general store was larger than the other buildings on the green. A counter ran along the back. Behind the counter a man stood at an old-fashioned cash register, ringing up purchases. All the walls of the store held shelves from floor to ceiling, containing almost everything a person might need.

"This is like an old-fashioned supermarket," said Benny.

"Yes it is," Jessie agreed.

There were piles of cloth in all different patterns, spools of thread, bars of soap wrapped in brown paper, and candles like the ones the children had dipped the day before. There were shelves holding quill pens, jars of ink, sheets of parchment paper and envelopes tied together with ribbon, and sealing wax in many colors. In one corner was a rack of brooms and in another corner a large pile of handwoven baskets. Near the door was a case containing boxes of biscuits, tins of tea and coffee, jugs of maple syrup, and jars of jam.

But what caught Benny's eye was the line of large glass jars on the counter. Each jar held a different kind of candy: long strings of licorice, red and white striped peppermint sticks, sour lemon drops.

"That peppermint candy looks good," said Benny, eyeing the red-and-white striped sticks.

"Benny! We haven't even had lunch yet," Henry said.

"I know," said Jessie. "We'll buy some candy now and then we'll go have lunch at the snack bar. We can save the candy for dessert."

The children selected some candy: a peppermint stick for Benny, a cinnamon stick for Henry, and licorice for Jessie and Violet. They also bought some sour lemon drops for Grandfather, since those were his favorite.

Then the children went to the snack bar and ate hot dogs and french fries.

"Do you think Shelly has gotten the shipment of clay yet?" Benny asked as he popped his last bite of hot dog in his mouth and licked the mustard off his fingers.

"I don't know," Henry said, gathering up their paper napkins and throwing them in the garbage. "Let's go find out."

The Aldens headed across the green, chewing on licorice and sucking on candy sticks.

As they started down the path toward the pottery shop, they heard loud voices. But it wasn't until they got to the door of the pottery shop that they realized the voices belonged to Eric and Shelly, who were inside. And they didn't sound happy.

"You're making a big mistake," said Eric angrily.

"*I'm* not. *You* are," Shelly insisted.

"I'll do this my way," Eric replied.

The children stood right outside the door of the shop trying to decide if they should enter or go away. They knew it wasn't right to eavesdrop on other people's conversations. But they couldn't help wondering what the two were talking about. Why were they so angry?

Shelly was just starting to say something when Benny dropped the bag of sour lemon drops, and it clattered to the ground noisily. He hurried to pick up the bag, but it was too late. Shelly and Eric had heard.

"What was that?" asked Shelly, looking toward the door.

The Aldens had no choice now but to enter the pottery shop.

"Hello," Henry said, going inside with Jessie and Violet behind him. Benny quickly picked up the candies and followed.

Eric looked very upset to see the children. "I'll talk to you later," he said over his shoulder to Shelly. He walked quickly out the door.

"How nice of you to drop by," Shelly said.

"Has the new shipment of clay come in yet?" Jessie asked.

"No, I'm afraid it hasn't," said Shelly. "But do you have any questions about pottery that I could answer?"

The children had a lot of questions for Shelly, but they weren't about pottery. They wanted to ask what she and Eric had been arguing about, but they knew they couldn't.

"No, thank you," Violet said politely. "We'll try back here later in the week."

The Aldens began walking out the door, when suddenly Benny turned around. "Would you like a sour lemon drop?"

Shelly smiled. "I would love one." Benny took the bag over to her and she put her hand in and pulled out a candy. Again the children noticed her bright red fingernails.

When the children were outside, Jessie said quietly, "What do you think Eric and Shelly were arguing about?"

"I don't know," said Violet, "but they sounded very upset."

"They certainly didn't sound as if they'd just met a few days ago," Henry pointed out.

"You know what I'm wondering," said Violet. "Did you notice Shelly's fingernails? They looked awfully nice for someone who usually has her hands covered with clay."

"Good point," Henry said. "I never would have thought of that."

"Remember she didn't seem to know much about pottery the other day," Jessie added. "Maybe she isn't really a potter at all."

"Then why is she pretending to be one?" Henry wondered aloud.

Since no one knew the anwer to this question, Jessie spoke up. "I think it's time we took a break. Let's go over to Grandfather's hotel for a swim."

"Great idea," Henry said.

"Yeah!" said Benny.

The children went back to their cabin and changed out of their colonial costumes and into regular clothes. Then they gathered their bathing suits.

They went to Linda's office to call Grandfather and tell him they were on their way.

"I'll meet you later at the tavern for dinner," Linda said.

"That's great!" Jessie said.

The children walked the short distance from Pilgrim Village to the hotel. It felt strange to be back in the modern world, where everyone dressed in modern clothes and there were electric lights and cars. Grandfather met them at the swimming pool. The children gave Grandfather the sour lemon drops they had bought for him. Then they all got into the pool, and splashed and dived and raced each other back and forth. Even Grandfather joined in.

CHAPTER 7

Peanut Butter and Jelly, Please

When it was time for dinner, they went to Grandfather's room to put on dry clothes. Then they all walked back to the village together.

The Aldens arrived at the tavern and sat at a large table near the kitchen. When they looked up at the menu written on the chalkboard, they were surprised to see that many items had been crossed off. Only fish chowder, roast beef, and baked ham remained.

Linda showed up a few minutes later and Steve came over to take their order.

"No chicken pot pie tonight?" Grandfather asked, disappointed.

"Sorry," Steve said. "We're all out."

"It looks like you're out of a lot of things," Linda commented. "What's going on?"

"I don't know," said Steve. "Busy night, I guess."

As they were speaking, Lisa came out of the kitchen and went to the chalkboard. She crossed roast beef off the menu.

"Oh, no," said Violet. Several people sitting at other tables groaned also. "I was going to order roast beef."

"Is there *anything* left?" Benny asked.

"Fish chowder and baked ham," Steve said.

"I don't want either one," Benny said sadly.

Linda looked thoughtfully at Benny. "Steve, would you ask Red to come out here, please?"

"Sure," Steve said, hurrying to the kitchen. A moment later, Red was walking toward their table.

"What's going on, Red?" Linda asked him.

"Didn't you order enough food this week?"

"Yes, I did," Red grumbled. "I guess I was so busy with — " He stopped abruptly. "All I know is, we suddenly ran out." He looked angry.

"Well, maybe you could make something special for this hungry boy." Linda put her arm around Benny. "What would you like?"

"Peanut butter and jelly, please," said Benny.

"We don't usually serve it, but I'll see if I have some in the kitchen."

"The rest of us will have baked ham," Grandfather said.

"All right," Red said, starting to go back to the kitchen.

"Red, I'd like you to come by my office tomorrow," Linda said. "We may have to make some changes around here."

"I'll come to your office," Red said, "but this is my kitchen, and I'll run it the way I see fit." With that he turned angrily and walked into the kitchen.

Linda sighed heavily. "If it's not one thing, it's another."

"Has anything like this ever happened before?" Henry asked.

"No, not that I can recall," replied Linda.

"I wonder what Red's been so busy with," Jessie said. "It sounded as if he started to say something and then changed his mind."

"He also said that the supplies ran out 'suddenly.' Do you think someone could have stolen the food?" asked Henry.

"Why would someone steal food?" Linda said.

"I don't know. Maybe to cause trouble, like they did at the weaving shop," Henry suggested.

Linda looked doubtful.

Soon Steve brought their food, and the table grew silent as Benny gobbled up his sandwich hungrily, and everyone else ate the baked ham. When they were finished they were glad to find that the kitchen hadn't run out of ice cream.

"Despite the problems, I'm happy to say that was another delicious dinner," Grandfather remarked as he and Linda walked the children back to their cabin.

"Yes," Linda mumbled. But she didn't seem happy at all.

"What's wrong?" Violet asked.

"Oh, it's just that things were going so well for Pilgrim Village. And now, in the last few days, everything seems to be going wrong," Linda said. "And with Thanksgiving coming I'm especially worried."

"There have been a lot of things going wrong," Jessie agreed.

"Just in the last few days?" Henry asked thoughtfully.

"Yes," Linda said. "I wish I knew what was going on, or who was doing it, or why." She seemed very sad. Everyone was silent for a moment.

"Don't worry," Benny said at last. "We're good at solving mysteries. We'll figure it out."

"I don't know if you can, but I hope so. Good night." Linda walked off in the darkness toward her office.

"Here's your cabin," Grandfather said. "I'd better be heading back to my hotel. I'll see you all tomorrow."

"Good night, Grandfather," the children called out as they lit their lantern and went into the cozy cabin.

As soon as they'd all changed into their pajamas, Jessie asked everyone to come sit in her and Violet's room. "I think we need to talk about what's been going on here," she said.

"We have to do something to help Linda," Violet said.

"Yes," Henry agreed. "Let's think of all the things that have happened, and see if we can figure out any pattern."

One by one, the children listed the strange happenings.

"First there were the mixed-up letters on our poster," said Violet.

"And the burnt biscuits," said Henry.

"The mess in the weaving shop and the ruined clay in the pottery shop," said Jessie.

"Don't forget the pin Violet found in the wax," Benny added.

"These don't seem to be things a thief would do," said Henry. "It just seems as if

someone wants to cause trouble."

"But who?" asked Benny.

"Eric and Shelly have both acted very strangely," Jessie said. "They pretended they'd never met, but I think they had. Eric is friendly one minute and trying to get rid of us the next."

"And Shelly doesn't really seem to know anything about pottery," added Violet.

"What about Red? He hasn't been very nice to us," said Benny.

"Remember the first night we were here, Red said the village was too crowded?" Henry said. "Maybe he's trying to cause trouble to get rid of some of the visitors."

"Maybe, but that doesn't explain how strangely Shelly and Eric are acting," said Violet.

"Shelly just started working here, and suddenly there are all these strange things happening," said Benny.

"I keep wondering if Eric's 'project' has anything to do with what's been happening," said Jessie.

Everyone sat and thought about that for a minute.

"There's only one way to find out," Henry said, finally. And then he told the others his plan.

CHAPTER 8

Henry's Plan

The next morning, after a quick breakfast of muffins and juice, the children went to the print shop. The shop looked empty, but the sign on the door said "Open" and there was a light on in Eric's office at the back.

"Hello," Jessie called out.

"Well, hello," Eric replied, emerging from his office.

"We wanted to see what you were working on today," Jessie said.

"I'm printing some signs for the general store," Eric told them. "Come over here and I'll show you."

Jessie, Violet, and Benny followed Eric over to the counter. But Henry did not. Instead, he quickly ducked into Eric's office to take a look around. He knew probing around like this wasn't exactly a nice thing to do. But the Aldens had decided it was important to help Linda. There on the desk was just what the Aldens had been wondering about — the old book with the cracked leather cover.

Peeking out into the main room to be sure Eric was busy, Henry picked up the book and looked at the first page. "Oh, my gosh," he said when he saw what was written there in thin, spidery handwriting.

The Journal of Thomas S. Heathcliff
begun January 5, 1780

"So that's what this old book is," Henry muttered to himself. He looked quickly at the page of notes Eric had been making.

Eric's handwriting was messy and hard to read. But at the top, Henry saw:

G. Washington to T. Heathcliff, February 1780

Suddenly Henry heard Eric say his name in the other room.

"Where's Henry?" Jessie repeated. She was speaking extra loudly so that Henry would be sure to hear. It was sort of a warning. "Oh he's — "

Just then there was a loud crash.

"Oh, Benny, you've knocked over a case of type!" said Violet.

"Sorry!" Benny said. But he didn't sound very sorry at all.

"That's okay," Eric said. "We'll all help put the type back in the right compartments."

Henry knew that his little brother had knocked the case of type over on purpose, to distract Eric.

Realizing he didn't have much time, Henry quickly looked back at the desk. Be-

side Eric's notes was a map of Pilgrim Village, the one given out to the visitors so they could find their way around. In blue pen, Eric had circled six buildings: the print shop, the weaver's shop, the candlemaker's shop, the tavern, the farmhouse, and the little cabin that the children were staying in, which used to be the guest cabin.

Henry noticed that those buildings were all tinted gray on the map, while the other buildings were black. He looked for the map's key to find out why. The key was in the corner. It said that the black buildings were all built recently, while the gray buildings were built back when Thomas Heathcliff was alive. Eric had circled all of the old buildings.

Henry had to leave before Eric realized that he had been in his office. He wasn't sure what he had learned from his detective work. But he knew that when he talked to his brother and sisters, they'd figure out something.

He peeked back into the main room of the print shop, and saw that everyone was kneeling on the floor, picking up the blocks of type that Benny had knocked onto the floor. Jessie caught Henry's eye and motioned for him to hurry.

Before Eric could turn around, Henry slipped into the room. No one but Jessie even noticed.

A little while later the children were back in their cabin. Henry was telling them what he had found.

"So the old book was Thomas Heathcliff's journal. I'd love to see what it says," said Violet. "I wonder why Eric is being so secretive with it."

"What do you think his notes meant, 'G. Washington to T. Heathcliff, February, 1780,' " Jessie wondered.

"I don't know. And I also don't know why he circled all the old buildings on the map," said Henry.

"Something strange has happened in each of those places," said Violet.

"Except for the farmhouse and our cabin," said Jessie.

"Is Eric trying to destroy Pilgrim Village?" Violet asked, her face sad.

"I don't know," said Jessie.

"I hope not," Violet said. "He seems so nice."

"We wanted a mystery," Benny said, "and we got one!"

The children had a picnic lunch with Grandfather on the green. Then they spent the afternoon visiting the little schoolhouse. They sat on hard wooden benches while a woman explained what school was like in the old days. Back then, children of all different ages were in the same class. The littlest children, like Benny, sat in the front row, while the older children, like Henry, were in the last.

Seeing the old school was lots of fun, and it almost made the Aldens forget about the mystery they were trying to solve. But as soon as they returned to their cabin, they remembered. Because in the middle of the table they found something mysterious. It was a note, written in large handwriting with lots of fancy loops and swirls.

"What does it say?" Benny asked when Jessie had picked it up.

"It says," Jessie began, reading aloud: " '*Meet me tonight at six-thirty at the farmhouse. I have something important to show you. I may be late — please wait for me.*' And it's signed '*Eric.*' "

"Something important," Benny repeated. "Wow!"

"Could I see it, please?" asked Henry. Jessie handed him the note.

"Do you think this has something to do with Eric's 'special project?' " asked Violet.

"Maybe," said Jessie.

"I don't know," Henry said after studying the note. "Something just doesn't feel right."

"Do you think we should tell Linda?" asked Violet.

"No, she has enough on her mind right now," said Jessie. "Let's wait and see what Eric has to show us first."

It was already almost six o'clock. The children ate a quick pizza dinner at the snack bar, and then walked to the farmhouse. Eric wasn't there yet, so they sat down on the front porch to wait for him. Most of the shops in the village had closed for the night, and there weren't many visitors around.

Soon it began to grow dark. Everything was quiet, and there were shadows everywhere. Far off in the distance an owl hooted.

Benny shivered. "Where's Eric?" he asked.

"I don't know," said Jessie. "But he said he might be late. I'm sure he'll be here any minute now."

Several more minutes passed, and still there was no sign of Eric.

"Do you think he's coming?" asked Violet.

"Maybe we should stop by the print shop and see if he's there," Henry suggested.

So the children walked slowly around the green to the print shop. But when they got there they saw that the lights had been turned off, and the door was shut tight. The sign in the window said "Closed." There was no sign of Eric.

"Oh, well, let's go back to our cabin. We

can come here tomorrow and ask Eric what he was planning to show us," Jessie said sensibly.

"Good idea," Henry said.

As they walked back to the cabin, Henry grew quiet. Suddenly he turned to Jessie. "Let me see that note again."

Jessie handed him the note, and Henry looked at it quickly. "That's what's wrong. This isn't Eric's handwriting."

"It isn't? How do you know?" asked Benny.

"I saw his notes about Thomas Heathcliff's journal," Henry reminded them. "Eric's handwriting was small and messy. This handwriting is big and fancy."

"Are you saying you don't think Eric wrote this note?" asked Jessie.

"That's right," said Henry. "Someone else did. Someone who wanted us to be at the farmhouse tonight."

"But why?" Violet wanted to know. "Nothing was happening there."

The children walked along, trying to think of an answer to Violet's question.

Suddenly Jessie stopped walking. "Maybe this has nothing to do with the farmhouse."

The others stopped walking also, and looked at her.

"What do you mean, Jessie?" Violet asked slowly.

"Maybe someone just wanted to get us out of our cabin!" Jessie exclaimed.

The children all stared at her for a minute, and then realized what that meant.

"Oh, my gosh," exclaimed Violet.

"Let's go!" Henry cried out.

The children took off, running as fast as they could back to their cabin.

When they got there, it was just as they had feared. The door of the cabin was open slightly. Someone had gone inside while they were away.

Henry quickly lit the lantern. When he saw the state of the cabin he gasped and stepped backward.

"What is it?" Jessie asked. Then her mouth dropped open as she saw what had made Henry gasp.

The cabin was a complete mess. Someone

had turned over all the furniture, torn the sheets and quilts off the bed, and dumped everything on the floor.

"Oh no," Violet said. "Who could have done such a terrible thing?"

CHAPTER 9

Who Wrote the Note?

The Aldens had no idea who would have made such an awful mess in their cabin.

"Should we go inside and clean it up?" Benny asked, hoping the answer would be no.

"I think we'd better go tell Linda first," said Jessie.

The Aldens went next door to Linda's office. She was sitting at her desk, working on a pile of papers. She glanced up and motioned to the children to come in, before going back to what she was working on.

"I'm just finishing a letter I was writing," she said without looking up. "I saw you in the little schoolhouse. Did you enjoy it?"

Their visit to the schoolhouse seemed very long ago to the children.

"Yes," Henry said. "But something awful has happened since then."

Linda looked up quickly. Now she saw the serious expressions on the children's faces. "What's wrong? What's happened?"

"It started with this note," Jessie began, handing the note to Linda.

She read it quickly and then looked up. "Yes?"

"We went to the farmhouse to meet Eric, but he never showed up. So we went back to our cabin." Jessie took a deep breath, trying to think of a gentle way to break the bad news to Linda.

But before she could, Benny burst out, "And it was wrecked!"

"Benny!" Jessie said.

"Well, it was," Benny insisted.

"Wrecked?" Linda repeated. "What do you mean?"

"Someone sent us this note to get us out of our cabin," Henry explained. "And while we were gone, they came in and turned over all the furniture."

"They took the sheets and blankets off the beds and everything!" Benny said.

"It looks the way the weaver's shop looked yesterday," Violet said.

Linda shook her head. "I'd better go see," Linda said grimly, getting up from her desk and leading the way back to the cabin.

Linda was just as stunned as the children had been when they entered the cabin. "This *is* awful! Who would do such a thing?" She sighed heavily.

"Whoever did it sent us the note to get us out of the way," Jessie explained.

"Wait a minute," Linda said. "Isn't the note from Eric?"

"That's what it says on it," Henry said. "But that's not Eric's handwriting."

"Let me see that note again," Linda said. Jessie gave it to her, and Henry handed her the lantern. She looked at it briefly. "You're right. Eric's handwriting is so messy I usually can't even read it. When he leaves me messages I never know what they say." Linda looked up. "But if this note isn't from Eric, then who is it from? And why does it say Eric on it?"

"Someone wanted us to *think* Eric had written it," Violet said.

Linda looked around the messy cabin and sighed again. "Now what?" she muttered to herself.

Just then they heard a knock on the front door, and Grandfather poked his head in. "Hello!" he called out, a big smile on his face. But as soon as he saw the mess inside the cabin, his smile disappeared. "What happened here?" he asked.

Henry quickly explained.

"I think it's time to call the police, Linda," Grandfather said. "These 'pranks' — or whatever you want to call them — have gone far enough."

"But if people hear about what's going on and see the police here, it will be terrible for

Pilgrim Village," Linda said. "I just don't know what to do."

The Aldens felt sorry for Linda. She looked so sad.

"For starters, we'll clean up in here," Jessie said, "and we'll see if anything is broken, or missing."

Linda smiled weakly. "You kids are great. I don't know what I'd do without you."

Linda and the Aldens began to straighten up the cabin. Violet picked up the things that were on the floor, while Henry and Grandfather set the furniture upright. Jessie and Benny made the beds with fresh linens. Linda checked to make sure that nothing was broken or missing.

At last things were back in order. "The good news is nothing was stolen," Linda said after she'd checked everything. "Whoever did this just wanted to cause trouble."

"I have another idea," said Violet. "Maybe they were looking for something. Did you notice that some of the loose stones in the fireplace were pulled out?"

"What would they be looking for?" Linda wondered aloud.

"If anyone can get to the bottom of a mystery, my grandchildren can," said Grandfather. "But right now, I think we could all use a good night's sleep." Grandfather tucked one arm around Benny and the other around Violet. "I think all of you should come back to the hotel with me."

"Good idea, James," said Linda. "I'll see you tomorrow morning for breakfast at the tavern."

After Linda left, the Aldens gathered their suitcases and went with Grandfather back to his hotel. The whole way there they talked about all the mysterious things that had been happening at Pilgrim Village, and wondered who was to blame.

"I've been thinking about what Linda said," Jessie said. "She didn't want to call the police because she was afraid the bad publicity for the village would frighten visitors away. Maybe that's what someone wants."

"I don't know," Henry said. "I think the

person is looking for something. And I think Thomas Heathcliff's journal may be the clue."

"What's this about Thomas Heathcliff's journal?" Grandfather asked.

"We saw Eric reading it, but he didn't seem to want us to know what it was," Violet explained.

"I see," Grandfather said. "Well this mystery solving is too much for me. I'll leave it to you young people."

They were almost at the hotel when Benny felt some raindrops sprinkling on his face. Soon the other Aldens also noticed that it was drizzling.

"They've predicted a big storm for tonight," Grandfather said. "We'd better hurry if we don't want to get soaked."

No sooner had he said that than there was a crash of thunder and rain began pouring down on them. "Hurry!" Henry called out, motioning to the others.

They all ran as quickly as they could. But they were still soaking wet by the time they reached the hotel. The children stood in the lobby shivering while Grandfather arranged for the children to have the two rooms across the hall from his.

A little while later the Aldens were warm and dry, Grandfather in his room, Henry and Benny in another room, and Jessie and Violet in the third. They had all taken hot baths and changed into warm, dry pajamas, before slipping into their beds. They fell asleep to the sound of raindrops pattering on the windows.

CHAPTER 10

Benny Saves the Day

When the children woke up they were happy to see that the rain had stopped, and the day was bright and sunny. They dressed in their colonial costumes before meeting Grandfather in the lobby. Together they walked back to the village to have breakfast at Red's Tavern.

"We've been so busy thinking about this mystery, I'd almost forgotten that we're going home tomorrow," Henry pointed out.

"We are?" asked Benny.

"Yes. We've been here a week," Grandfather said.

"Then we've got to solve this mystery today!" said Violet.

"I thought we had more time," Benny said. "I'm going to miss this place."

"What will you miss most?" Jessie asked.

Benny thought for a moment. "The horses." They had just reached the village. Benny grabbed Grandfather's hand and tugged on it. "Grandfather, can I go visit the horses right now?"

"Before breakfast?" Grandfather asked.

"Just for a few minutes," Benny said. "Please?"

"All right," said Mr. Alden. "Don't stay too long though."

Benny ran off immediately, his three-cornered hat bouncing up and down on his head. The other Aldens smiled as they looked after him, before heading to the tavern for breakfast.

* * *

Benny reached the stable a few minutes later. Because of the rainstorm the night before, the yard was full of mud, and there were lots of loose stones where the dirt had been washed away. Benny ran ahead, eager to see the horses.

All of a sudden, he slipped on some mud and fell down.

"Ouch!" Benny muttered as his knee hit something sharp. He looked to see what he had landed on. It felt much sharper than a rock.

"There it is," Benny said to himself. Something dark and pointy stuck up out of the muddy ground. Benny looked closer.

He'd thought it was a rock, but now he saw that it was metal. It looked like the corner of a box.

"Oh, my gosh!" Benny cried out. "Buried treasure!" On his hands and knees, Benny began furiously pushing the dirt away from the metal box. As he dug down deeper, the dirt became too densely packed to move with his bare hands. Benny looked around. Off to

one side of the stable he found a large flat stone that he could use as a shovel.

At last Benny managed to uncover the square metal box. But he was very disappointed when he saw that the box was shut tight with a large metal lock.

"Wait until Henry and Jessie and Violet see this!" he cried, picking up the box and running all the way to the tavern.

Meanwhile, Linda and the Aldens were beginning to wonder what had happened to Benny.

"He certainly wouldn't miss breakfast," Jessie said.

"Not our Benny," Violet agreed.

At just that moment, Benny ran in, out of breath and covered with mud.

"Look at you!" Henry said.

"What have you been up to?" asked Jessie.

Then the Aldens saw the box Benny was carrying.

"What's that?" Violet asked.

Benny had almost caught his breath. "It's buried treasure," he gasped. "I found it in the stable yard!"

Linda and the Aldens gathered around Benny, who placed the rusty old box on the table.

"Well would you look at that," Linda said, almost to herself.

"What do you think is inside?" Violet asked.

"Only one to way to find out," said Jessie.

"But it's locked," Benny said.

"That lock looks pretty rusty and weak to me. All we need is a hammer to pry it off," said Henry.

"There's one in my office," Linda said.

"What have you got there?" asked Red, who had just come out of the kitchen. He was looking at the box with great interest.

"Buried treasure!" cried Benny.

"I don't know, Red," said Linda. "Benny just found this in the stable yard, and we're going back to my office to find out what it is. Join us if you'd like," Linda said.

Red looked around the tavern, which was unusually empty. "Things seem pretty quiet here. I think I will join you."

With Benny carrying the box, Linda led

the group back to her office. She got out her hammer and placed the back end of it in the lock and pushed down hard. Slowly, slowly, the weak, rusty metal lock began to give. At last it snapped off.

She pushed the box toward Benny. "It's your treasure."

Benny lifted the top of the metal box. But when he saw what was inside, he was disappointed. "There's no treasure in here. There's just a piece of paper." He lifted a folded, yellowed piece of paper from the box.

"That's not just a piece of paper," a voice said.

Everyone looked up. Eric had just come in and was peering around the group at what Benny was holding. "It's a map," he said.

"A treasure map?" Benny asked excitedly.

"Not the kind you're thinking of," Eric said, "but the map itself is a treasure. A very old, historic treasure."

Carefully Benny unfolded the piece of paper. Eric was right. It was a map.

"Where did you find it?" Eric asked Benny.

"It was in this metal box, buried in the yard by the stable," Benny said. "I saw a corner sticking up out of the mud."

"But how did you know what was in the box?" Jessie asked.

"Does this have something to do with your special project?" asked Violet.

"Yes, as a matter of fact, it does," Eric said. "I've been wondering where this was hidden. May I?" He gestured to Benny, who nodded. Very carefully, Eric took the map in his hands and looked at it. A warm smile filled his face.

"Would you mind explaining what you're talking about?" Linda asked.

"It's a long story," Eric began. "You see, my, uh, assistant and I were studying Thomas Heathcliff's journal. In it, he mentions a visit by George Washington in February of 1780. He says that Washington, who was the commander of the Revolutionary Army, gave him a hand-drawn map of an upcoming battle. Heathcliff wrote in his journal that he hid the map somewhere on the farm."

Eric paused and looked around at everyone. They were watching him and listening, fascinated.

"Go on," said Linda.

"Well, the map has never been found. My assistant and I realized that it must still be hidden here somewhere. And . . ." Eric didn't seem to know what to say next.

"And you've been looking for it," Jessie finished for him.

"It's a bit more complicated than that," said Eric. "I wanted to find the map and display it here at the village. It's a wonderful, important piece of history, and people should be able to see it."

"Think of all the visitors it would bring," Linda said.

"Exactly," Eric agreed. "But my assistant had a different idea. She thought that if we found it we should sell it to a big museum. All she was interested in was making money. I told her I couldn't agree to that. And so she stormed off."

"Are you talking about Judith?" asked Jessie.

"No, not my shop assistant," Eric said. "My *research* assistant."

"Is someone talking about me?" asked a voice.

Everyone turned to see Shelly standing in the doorway.

"Yes," Eric said to Shelly. "Benny found the map."

"Would somebody please tell me what's going on?" Red asked, completely confused.

Now Shelly took up the story. She sounded weary. "I guess Eric has told you that we both wanted to find the map. I took the potter's job just so that I could sneak into the old buildings and look for the map after hours."

"We figured out that you weren't really a potter," said Jessie.

"I've never made a pot in my life," Shelly said. "I read some books so that I could answer questions, but I would never have been able to make a pot. That's why I had to get rid of all the clay."

"We also knew that you and Eric hadn't just met that day on the green," Henry said.

"That was when I realized what Shelly was up to," Eric said. "And I knew I had to find the map before she did."

"So you read Heathcliff's journal for clues, and planned to search in all the original buildings," Henry said.

"Yes," Eric said.

"I knew that you were looking, too," said Shelly, "so I hurried to find the map first. In my rush I made some mistakes."

"Like knocking over our tray of type in the printer's shop?" asked Benny.

"Yes. I didn't have time to fix it so I just threw the blocks back in the tray any which way," Shelly said.

"And then you looked in the candlemaker's shop," Violet said.

"How did you know that?" Shelly asked.

"Violet found your pin in the wax. I knew it looked familiar. You were wearing it on your blouse the day we met you," Jessie said.

"Is that where I lost it?" said Shelly. "It must have fallen off while I was searching there. Then I looked in the weaver's shop."

"And you made quite a mess," said Linda angrily.

"I know," Shelly said, looking sad. "Finding the map had become the most important thing to me. I was frantic."

"And you sent us that note that was supposed to be from Eric, just to get rid of us," said Jessie.

"I had to search your cabin," said Shelly.

"And all along the map was buried in the stable yard," said Eric.

"Why didn't you tell me about this map, Eric?" Linda demanded.

"I should have," Eric admitted. "I didn't want to get your hopes up since I wasn't sure it would really turn up. But when I saw all the trouble Shelly was causing, I came here this morning to tell you."

"Are you going to call the police?" Shelly asked Linda.

"I should," Linda said. "What you've done was very selfish and wrong. But bad publicity won't help the village." Linda thought for a minute. "Shelly, you and I need to have a serious talk. I think we'll be able to figure out some way that you can repay the village for all the trouble you've caused."

Shelly nodded silently.

"What about the strange things happening at the tavern?" Jessie asked Shelly. "The burnt biscuits, and the food running out. Did you cause those, too?"

Shelly looked puzzled. "What are you talking about?"

Red cleared his throat. "I'm afraid those were my fault."

"*Your* fault?" Linda asked.

"Yes," Red said, sighing wearily. "I haven't wanted to admit it, but I just can't keep up with things the way I used to. Especially not with all the crowds lately. I'm afraid I messed up a few times lately."

"I've been telling you for years we should get you some extra help in the kitchen," Linda said.

"I know. I just never wanted to admit that I needed help," Red said.

"Maybe we could help with lunch today," Jessie offered. "I've been wanting to find out how you make that delicious apple pie." She smiled at Red.

"Sounds good to me," Red said, giving the Aldens the first real smile they'd seen from him.

"We've solved a mystery, and now we get to make apple pie!" Benny cried. "What a great vacation!"

GERTRUDE CHANDLER WARNER discovered when she was teaching that many readers who like an exciting story could find no books that were both easy and fun to read. She decided to try to meet this need, and her first book, *The Boxcar Children*, quickly proved she had succeeded.

Miss Warner drew on her own experiences to write each mystery. As a child she spent hours watching trains go by on the tracks opposite her family home. She often dreamed about what it would be like to set up housekeeping in a caboose or freight car — the situation the Alden children find themselves in.

When Miss Warner received requests for more adventures involving Henry, Jessie, Violet, and Benny Alden, she began additional stories. In each, she chose a special setting and introduced unusual or eccentric characters who liked the unpredictable.

While the mystery element is central to each of Miss Warner's books, she never thought of them as strictly juvenile mysteries. She liked to stress the Aldens' independence and resourcefulness and their solid New England devotion to using up and making do. The Aldens go about most of their adventures with as little adult supervision as possible — something else that delights young readers.

Miss Warner lived in Putnam, Connecticut, until her death in 1979. During her lifetime, she received hundreds of letters from girls and boys telling her how much they liked her books.

YE OLDE ACTIVITY PAGES

When the Aldens visited Pilgrim Village, they learned a lot about life in colonial times. The kids back then had no TVs, no stereos, no video games. So what did they do for fun? Well, colonial kids weren't much different from you — they cooked, made things, and even tried their hands at a few puzzling puzzlers.

Where can you find some fun colonial things to make and do? No big Boxcar Children mystery there — the activities start on the very next page!

Unsolved Puzzle Mysteries

Kids in colonial times probably used a feather quill and an inkwell to solve their puzzles — but *you* can pull out a pencil or a ballpoint pen and start solving these tricky puzzlers!

Scrambled Sentence!

Jessie has spent all day arranging letters on the printing press. Now someone has messed them up! What did Jessie's message say? First unscramble the words, then put them in order, and you'll see.

A HREET'S OT YSERYMT EERH EWN VELSO ARXBOC

Colonial Words Wordsearch

Where can you find a buggy, a tourist, a churn, and candles? There are two answers to that question — at Pilgrim Village, and in this wordsearch! The words go up, down, sideways, and backwards. Look for: MYSTERY, CHURN, QUILTS, WAGON, NEWSPAPER, CANDLES, MARKET, BUGGY, INN, QUILL PEN, HORSES, TOURIST.

```
C  H  U  R  N  W  N  J  R  T  Q
I  A  A  C  N  A  A  E  L  O  U
S  Z  N  E  R  G  F  Q  P  U  I
E  N  E  D  K  O  F  U  A  R  L
S  Y  W  Y  L  N  H  I  Y  I  T
R  A  S  I  M  E  A  L  D  S  S
O  D  P  R  K  E  S  L  N  T  B
H  O  A  L  P  P  N  P  A  S  U
N  F  P  U  Y  P  N  E  C  T  G
A  B  E  C  A  B  I  N  S  E  G
A  B  R  O  T  E  K  R  A  M  Y
M  M  Y  S  T  E  R  Y  A  J  V
```

Crazy Candles!

Benny is so excited to be able to make a candle — and bring it home. But all the candles look alike. Which one is Benny's? Find the one that's different.

1   2   3   4   5

Transportation by the Numbers

There are no cars allowed at Pilgrim Village. So how do folks get around? Count by fours to connect the dots and you will see.

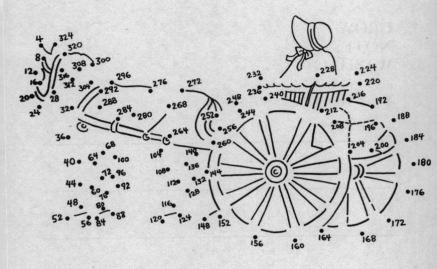

Lots of Letters

Pilgrim Village isn't far from one of General George Washington's headquarters during the Revolutionary War. How many words can you get from the letters in the words George Washington?

Don't worry. You're not alone in this. Henry's started you off with three words.

Henry's Words

GROW
NOTE
WASH

Your Words

_____

_____

_____

_____

_____

The Farmer's Market Memory Puzzle

The Boxcar Children will never forget their visit to the Pilgrim Village. But how much will you remember about this Farmer's Market scene? First color this picture. Then turn the page and take the memory test.

Circle the picture in each row that is the same as the one in the Farmer's Market scene on the previous page.

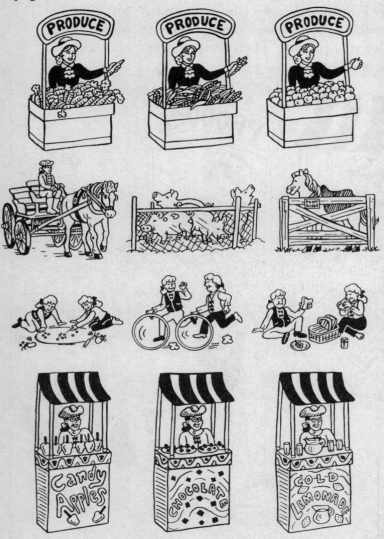

Rainy Days and Mazes

Oh no! It's pouring rain. The Aldens are very far from their little cabin at Pilgrim Village. Follow the maze and get them there as fast as you can!

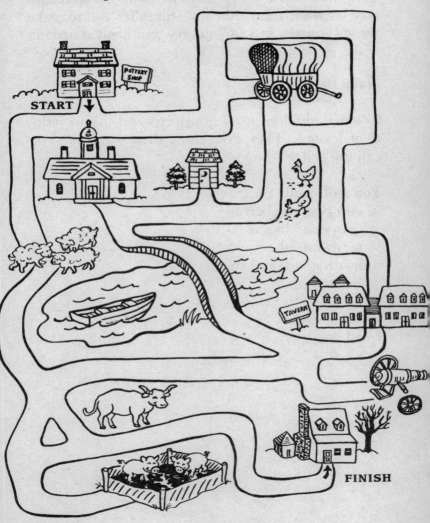

Colonial Crafts

Chores kept colonial children very busy. That's because colonial families had to make almost everything themselves. Nowadays we go to the store and buy what we need. But sometimes it's fun to make things yourself. So why not try *your* hand at making crafts *by* hand?

Make Berry Ink!

Colonial children used quill pens and ink to write their lessons. They even made their own ink. You can too. Here's how!

You will need:
½ cup ripe blueberries
½ teaspoon vinegar
½ teaspoon salt.
measuring cup and spoons
strainer
bowl
wooden spoon
small jar

Here's what you do:
Fill the strainer with the berries. Hold the strainer over the bowl. Use the rounded end of the wooden spoon to crush the berries against the strainer so the berry juice goes into the bowl. Keep adding berries until most of the juice has been strained out. Only berry juice should be in the bowl. Add the salt and vinegar to the berry juice. Stir in the salt and vinegar. Pour your ink into the jar. Make sure the jar is shut tight when the ink is not being used.

To write with your ink, dip a pointed twig or stick into the jar. You will probably have to dip the stick in the ink for each letter you write.

Here's a lesson colonial children had to learn. Try writing it with your berry ink.

He that ne'er learns his ABC
For ever will a blockhead be.

Super Silhouettes

Americans have been making silhouette portraits for centuries.

Back in colonial times, these shadow drawings were done by candlelight. Since this is the twentieth century, you can use a lightbulb.

You will need:
white drawing paper
a lamp with the shade removed
a chair
a pencil
tape
a black crayon
a friend or family member

Here's what you do:
Place the chair sideways against a blank wall. Ask the friend you are going to draw to sit in the chair. Place the lamp about ten feet from the wall, and at the same height as your friend's head. Tape the drawing paper just behind your friend's head, so that the shadow appears on the paper. Use the pencil to trace the shadow outline. Remember to remind your friend to sit very, very still.

Use the black crayon to color in the outline of your friend's shadow.

Friend of the Farmer

As far as Benny is concerned, the best part of Pilgrim Village is the food. It all tastes so fresh — especially since all the fruits and vegetables are grown right in the village.

The early settlers took their harvest very seriously. To this day, many New Englanders carry on a special harvest tradition. Each fall they build Harvest Dummies, just like the ones made by the early settlers. **Here's how you can make one, too:**

1. Gather together a pair of old jeans and a button-down, long-sleeved shirt.
2. Button the shirt, zip the pants, and stuff them both with old newspapers.
3. Stuff old gloves and socks with newspapers, too. Use safety pins to attach the gloves to the sleeves and the socks to the pants.
4. A paper bag makes a fine head. Draw the face on with markers or crayons. Then stuff the bag with old newspapers. An old mop or some yarn will do nicely as hair. Use safety pins or masking tape to attach the head to the shirt.
5. Place a straw hat on your Harvest Dummy's head. Then sit him on your porch and have him greet your harvest.

It's O-Clay With Violet!

Violet loved her visit to the village. She's only sorry she didn't get to make a clay pot to use back at Grandfather's house. But you can make things from clay any time you want. Here's how:

You will need:
1 cup all purpose flour
½ cup salt
⅓ cup water
food coloring
a mixing bowl

Here's what you do:
1. Mix the flour and salt together in a mixing bowl.
2. Add the water a little at a time. Use your hands to squeeze the clay until it is smooth.
3. Add a few drops of food coloring to your clay and keep squeezing until the food coloring is mixed in.

Store your clay in a plastic bag until you are ready to use it.

Puzzle Answers

Scrambled Sentence

THERE'S A NEW BOXCAR MYSTERY TO SOLVE HERE.

Colonial Word Wordsearch

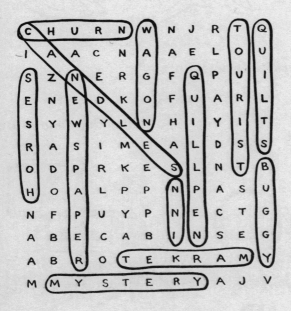

Crazy Candles

Number three is Benny's candle.

Transportation by the Numbers

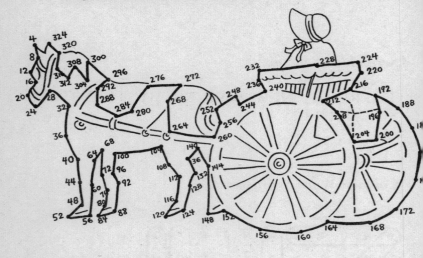

The Farmer's Market Memory Puzzle

Rainy Days and Maze

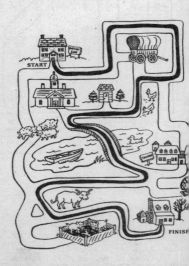